A MAGIC CIRCLE BOOK

The Unicorn and The Moon

written and illustrated by **TOMIE DE PAOLA**

THEODORE CLYMER
SENIOR AUTHOR, READING 360

GINN AND COMPANY
A XEROX EDUCATION COMPANY

The Unicorn and The Moon is a tale of today about strange creatures from stories of long ago.

The unicorn was a legendary animal somewhat like a small horse with a silver mane, and a long horn in the middle of its forehead.

The griffin, also legendary, was half-eagle and half-lion, a creature really frightful to see.

The alchemist was a man who studied chemistry and magic. He was supposed to have magic power and be able to change one thing into another.

And so our story begins one evening long ago just as the first star awakens a very beautiful unicorn.

The Unicorn was very beautiful, and because she was so beautiful, she was a little vain. She would go to the pool in her forest glade and admire herself reflected in its crystal clear waters. But nothing made the beauty of the Unicorn shine as did the moonlight.

That evening when the first star began to twinkle in the sky, the Unicorn awakened. Quickly she looked up at the sky to find the moon so she could go and stand in its light. But there was no moon.

"That's strange," she said. "The moon was out last night. I wonder where it is now."

Looking around and seeing a far-off glow like moonlight, the Unicorn set out to greet the moon as it rose.

She found the moon at last, but not in the sky. It was trapped between two hills.

"Moon, what are you doing there?" she asked.

"Late in the night when I was setting, I did not watch where I was going and these two hills caught me," answered the poor moon.

"Let the moon go," the Unicorn said to the hills.

"No!" answered the hills. "The moonlight makes your beauty shine. We want to be beautiful too!" And, indeed, the two hills were glowing with beauty from the moon's light.

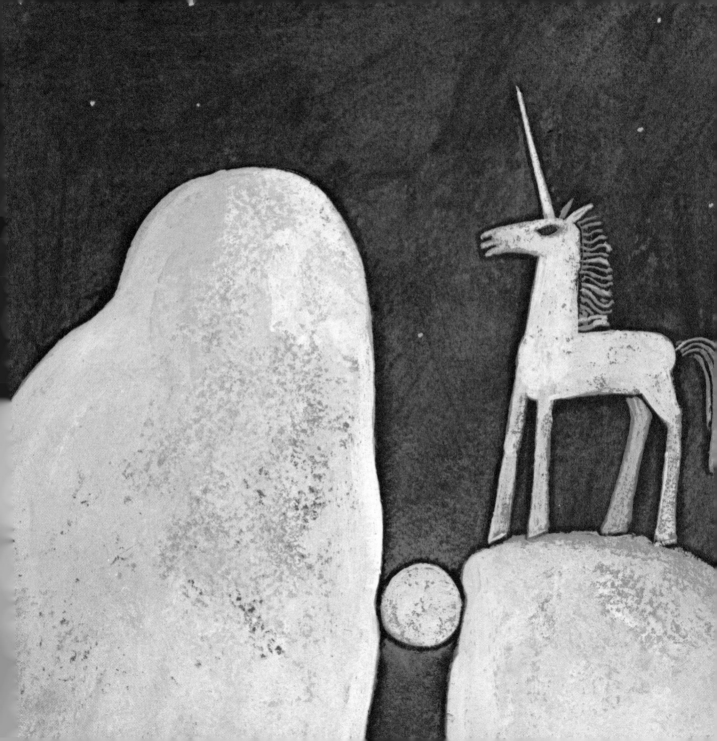

Now it was true that the Unicorn didn't need the moonlight because she glowed anyway. But she liked the way the moon made her seem even more beautiful.

"Let the moon go," she said again, "or I'll trample you until you let it go!"

"No," said the hills once more.

The Unicorn began to trample back and forth over the two hills. The more she trampled, the tighter the hills held together.

"Please stop," the moon called. "I'm being squeezed to death."

The Unicorn stopped and thought for a few minutes. Then she said to the moon, "I'll tickle you free with my horn."

14

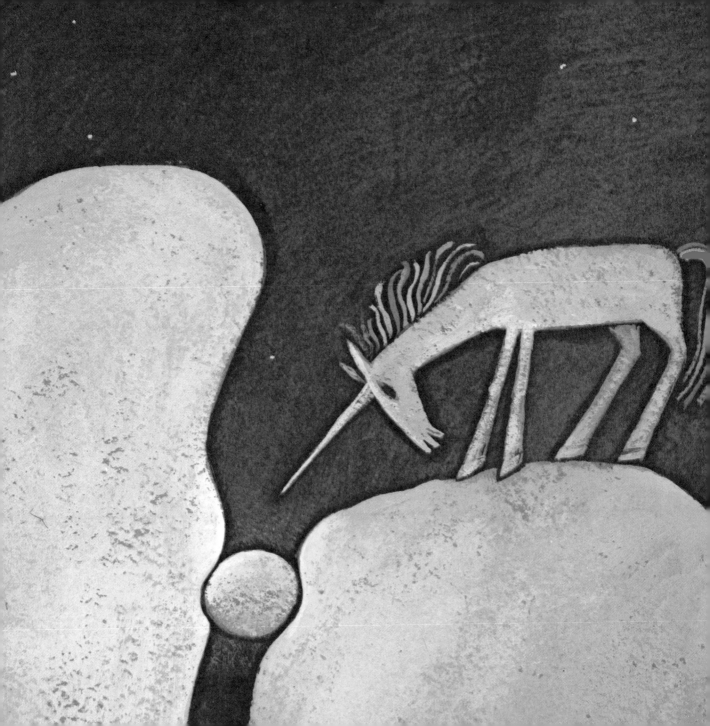

As she began to tickle the moon, it giggled and laughed and wiggled about. But the hills held together even tighter.

"Please stop, oh, please," begged the moon. "I'm being tickled to death."

The Unicorn stopped and thought for some time. Then she said, "I'll be right back. I'm going for help." And off she went to a dark cave deep in the forest.

"Griffin, oh, griffin, I need your help!" she called at the entrance to the cave.

The griffin appeared and was terrible to look at. But he was a friend of the Unicorn, so she was not afraid.

"What's the matter?" asked the griffin. And the Unicorn told him about the two hills that had trapped the moon.

"Of course I'll help," said the griffin, and he followed the Unicorn to the hills.

When they got there, the griffin roared and flapped his wings and whipped his tail around.

The two hills began to shake and tremble. So did the moon.

"We'll frighten you free," said the Unicorn.

"Oh, stop, please stop," cried the moon. "I'm being frightened and trembled to death."

The griffin stopped flapping his wings and whipping his tail around. "I'm sorry, Unicorn," he said, and he went back to his cave.

The Unicorn was very worried. There must be some way to free the moon!

"I'll have to ask my friend the alchemist for advice," she said. And away she ran as swift as starlight.

The alchemist was always busy trying to turn lead into gold. He had never succeeded, but in trying, he had learned many things. He was very smart.

"Unicorn," he said when he opened the door, "come in, come in. Have a cup of tea. What a nice surprise."

"I've no time. The moon is trapped!" she answered, and she told the alchemist the sad tale about the moon and the hills.

"Why don't you use your own magic?" asked the alchemist.

"I can only use it for myself," answered the Unicorn.

"That's true! Hmmmm, let me think," said the alchemist, scratching his head.

So the Unicorn waited while the alchemist worked on the problem. At last he told her what she must do.

The Unicorn returned to the hills, carrying a large bag. She dipped her nose into the bag and pulled out some round shiny objects which she began to toss high overhead. Suddenly the sky and the air all around were filled with moons — more moons than you could count using both hands.

"Look!" said the smaller of the two hills. "More moons! Let's catch them."

The hills began to reach for the other moons. As soon as they did, the real moon, free at last, shot up into the sky. The hills caught three new moons and held onto them as tightly as they could. The others fell to the ground.

"Why, they are mirrors!" exclaimed the moon.

"Shhh," said the Unicorn. "The hills aren't too smart. They'll never know if you don't tell them. And besides it doesn't matter. They look quite nice with just reflections of you."

"Oh, thank you for freeing me," said the moon.

"You're welcome," answered the Unicorn, whose beauty was now glowing brightly in the moonlight. "From now on be more careful when you're setting!"

"Oh, I will, I will," promised the moon.

"Well, I'm going to keep these," the Unicorn said, holding up the bag full of round mirrors, "just in case."

And she returned to her glade to shine in the moonlight and to look at herself in the crystal clear waters of the pool.

ABCDEFGHIJK 765432
PRINTED IN THE UNITED STATES OF AMERICA